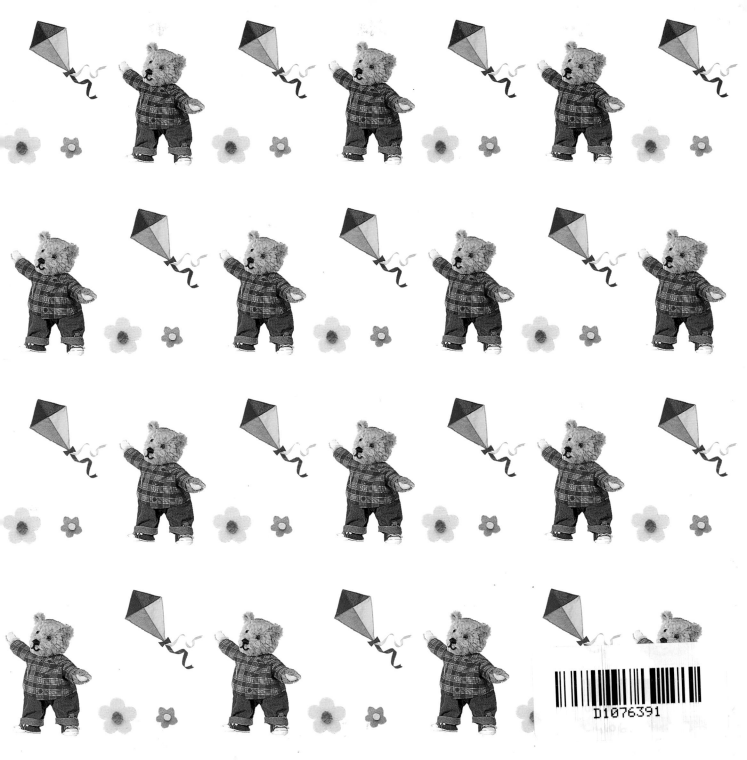

A DORLING KINDERSLEY BOOK

Senior Designer Claire Jones
Senior Editor Caryn Jenner
Editor Fiona Munro
Production Katy Holmes
Photography Dave King

First published in Great Britain in 1997
by Dorling Kindersley Limited,
9 Henrietta Street, London WC2E 8PS

Visit us on the World Wide Web at: http://www.dk.com

A CIP catalogue record for this book is available from the British Library.

ISBN 0 7513 7060 6

Reproduced in Italy by G.R.B. Graphica, Verona
Printed and bound in Italy by L.E.G.O.

Acknowledgments
Dorling Kindersley would like the thank the following
manufacturers for permission to photograph copyright material:
The Manhattan Toy Company for "Antique Rabbit"
Brio, Ltd. for the toy ducks

Dorling Kindersley would also like to thank
Vera Jones, Robert Fraser and Dave King
for their help with props and set design.

Can you find
the little bear
in each scene?

P.B. BEAR

Fly-Away Kite

Lee Davis

DORLING KINDERSLEY

LONDON • NEW YORK • STUTTGART • MOSCOW

It was a fine spring day. P.B. Bear packed
a picnic and went to meet his friend, Russell.
Across the field he went, then along the
bank of the stream to the bridge.
"Hello, Delilah," he called.
"Quack, quack," said Delilah Duck.
"Look at my new ducklings!"
P.B. Bear counted 1, 2, 3 ducklings
behind Delilah.

P.B. Bear saw Russell on the other side of the stream.
He ran across the bridge to meet his friend.
"Look what I've brought," said Russell.
"It's perfect weather to fly a kite."
P.B. Bear looked at the kite.
It had four colourful triangles,
one red tail,
one yellow tail,
and a big blue bow.
"But I don't know how to fly a kite," he said.
Russell started to unroll the string.
"I'll show you," he said.

P.B. Bear watched as Russell ran across
the field, holding tightly to the string.
The kite bounced along the ground
until SUDDENLY,
a helpful breeze blew it
up, up, up into the air.

"It's flying!"
shouted P.B. Bear.
"The kite is flying!"

"It's your turn now," said Russell.
P.B. Bear held the string carefully
and ran as fast as he could.

The kite fluttered
and floated into the sky
above the stream.
Higher and higher it went.
Delilah and her ducklings looked up at the kite.
"Quack, quack!" they cheered.

P.B. Bear ran and ran.
The faster he ran, the higher the kite flew!
P.B. Bear thought so hard about running,
that he forgot to hold onto the string.
The kite dipped and dived and drifted
lower and lower out of the sky.

"Quack! Look out, ducklings!" called Delilah,
as the kite fell into the stream with a SPLASH!

P.B. and Russell ran onto the bridge.
Together, they peered down at the stream.
The kite was floating in the water, just out of reach.
"Oh, Russell," said P.B. Bear sadly. "I'm sorry."

Delilah Duck picked
up the kite in her beak.
The first duckling picked up the red kite tail,
the second duckling picked up the yellow kite tail
and the third duckling picked up the string.
They all swam to the bridge.
"You've saved the kite!" said P.B. Bear. "Thank you."
"Quack, quack!" replied Delilah and her ducklings.

P.B. Bear shared the picnic with his friends.
"There's no harm done to the kite," said Russell.
"It will soon dry out in the sun, and then you
can have another turn."
"I'll keep hold of the string next time,"
        P.B. Bear promised.
         Russell tucked into the picnic.
      "Mmm, P.B., there is something that you
can do better than anyone else I know."
"Is there?" said P.B. Bear. "What's that?"
"Make a picnic lunch!" said Russell.
"Quack, quack!" agreed Delilah and the ducklings.

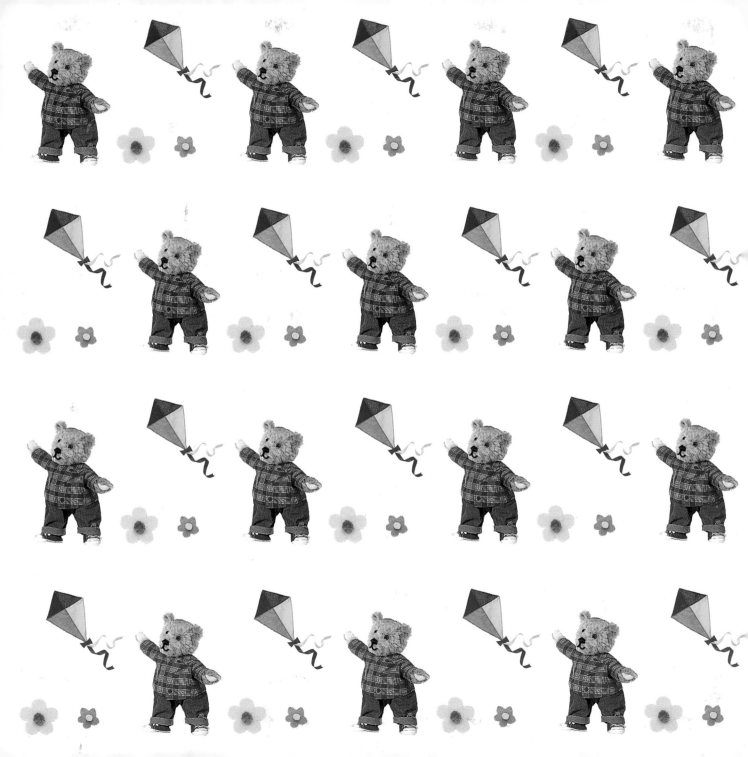